.

HEALTH WATCH

Heart Disease

Revised Edition

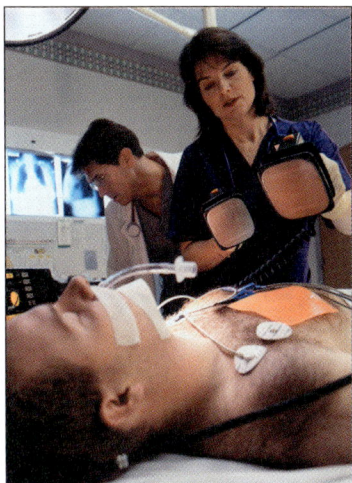

JOHN C. GOLD

*Expert Reviews by D. Joshua Cutler, M.D.,
Karen Uzark, Ph.D., R.N., and
Casey L. Draeger*

E

Enslow Publishers, Inc.

40 Industrial Road	PO Box 38
Box 398	Aldershot
Berkeley Heights, NJ 07922	Hants GU12 6BP
USA	UK

http://www.enslow.com

Acknowledgments

With thanks to:

D. Joshua Cutler, M.D., past president, American Heart Association, Maine Affiliate, for his advice and review of this book.

The American Heart Association, Maine Affiliate, for its help in collecting information for this book.

Dennis Dutremble for his willingness to share his story.

Printed in the United States of America. This is a revised edition of Heart Disease ©1996.

Library of Congress Cataloging-in-Publication Data

Gold, John C.

   Heart disease / John C. Gold; expert review by D. Joshua Cutler.

     p. cm. —— (Health watch) / Rev. ed.

Includes bibliographical references and index.

Summary: Describes the workings of the heart and the circulatory system and the array of ailments that can affect them, discussing symptoms, diagnosis, prevention, and treatment.

   ISBN 0-7660-1653-6

   1. Heart—Diseases—Juvenile literature. 2. Cardiovascular system—Juvenile literature. [1. Heart—Diseases. 2. Diseases. 3. Circulatory system.] I. Cutler, D. Joshua. II. Title. III. Health watch (Berkeley Heights, N.J.)

   RC673.H43 2000

   616.1′2—dc21

                                      00-008403

10 9 8 7 6 5 4 3 2 1

To Our Readers:

All Internet addresses in this book were active and appropriate when we went to press. Any comments or suggestions can be sent by e-mail to Comments@enslow.com or to the address on the back cover.

Illustration and Photo Credits:

© Digital Stock, Corbis Corp.: pp. 1, 22, 34; courtesy, Norton Audubon Heart Institute: pp. 4, 40; © PhotoDisc, Inc.: pp. 6, 17, 19, 20, 28; © Carl D. Walsh: p. 8; © Jill K. Gregory: pp. 11, 12, 13; courtesy, SCHILLER AG, Switzerland: p. 30; courtesy, Medtronic, Inc.: pp. 37, 38.

Cover Illustrations:

Large photo, © Digital Stock, Corbis Corp.; top inset, © Jill K. Gregory; bottom inset, © PhotoDisc, Inc.

Contents

William Schroder lived for almost two years with an artificial heart.

Heart Attack

I t was a Sunday night in the spring when Dennis Dutremble began feeling ill. He was sitting down because his back hurt. The backache got worse, so he decided to go to bed.

When he lay down in bed, things got worse. He could not breathe well. Suddenly his chest felt as if it had filled up with liquid. Terrible pain shot down his left arm. He thought he might die.

Mr. Dutremble's wife drove him to the hospital. He walked inside and leaned against the wall. He asked for help. Nurses rushed him into a room and put him on a bed. Then a doctor came. The medical staff connected Mr. Dutremble to a machine that measured his heartbeat.

The doctors told him he had suffered a heart attack. He was thirty-nine years old.

Mr. Dutremble's father had suffered two heart attacks. Mr. Dutremble's grandfather and uncle had both suffered **strokes**, another form of heart disease.

Mr. Dutremble was overweight. He smoked and

worked long, hard, stressful days as a state senator. Heart scientists say that being overweight, smoking, and feeling stressed can make a person more likely to have a heart attack.

Bypass Surgery

Mr. Dutremble lay in a hospital bed for two weeks, resting so his heart could recover. Doctors ran tests to find out how badly his heart was damaged. They found that fatty deposits were blocking three blood vessels that bring blood to the heart. As a result, parts of the heart served by these vessels did not receive enough oxygen to survive. When those parts died, Mr. Dutremble's heart weakened.

At the end of two weeks, Mr. Dutremble tried to walk down the hospital hall. It was too much work for his heart. He felt ill again. He had to be taken back to his bed in a wheelchair.

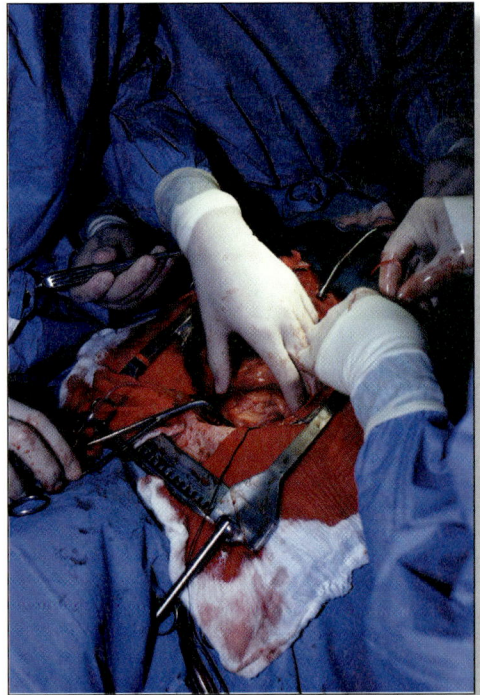

A surgical team performs open heart surgery.

The doctors conducted more tests on Mr. Dutremble. They told him that he would have to have surgery. The doctor also said that the damaged parts of Mr. Dutremble's heart might have to be removed and the heart sewn back together. The doctor told Mr. Dutremble he might never be able to work again.

During the surgery, called a coronary **bypass operation**, a surgeon cut open Mr. Dutremble's chest and then stopped his heart. A heart-lung machine pumped Mr. Dutremble's blood for him while his heart was stopped.

Once Mr. Dutremble's chest was opened, the surgeon built a new route for blood to flow through the heart. The new route bypassed the old, blocked vessels just as a highway bypass detours around a congested city.

During the operation, the surgeon used blood vessels from Mr. Dutremble's leg to bypass the clogged heart arteries. The surgeon also examined the heart and found that the damage was not as serious as the doctors had first thought.

But after his operation Mr. Dutremble was worried. Even though his heart was healthier than his doctors had thought, he feared he might die at a young age. He often listened to his heartbeat. He was afraid it might stop again.

Back to Work

Despite his worries, Mr. Dutremble recovered from his heart attack. He went back to work as a high school teacher and a state senator. His work schedule was busier than before his heart attack. He said he felt fine.

When the state legislature was in session, Mr. Dutremble sometimes worked as many as sixteen hours a day. He talked to people in his district or to other state officials,

Dennis Dutremble, accompanied by his wife, speaks to his supporters at a campaign rally as he runs for Congress seven years after his heart attack.

and he voted on proposed laws. On weekends he often met with voters or attended local events.

Regarding his schedule, he said, "I think it actually invigorates me. It's something I enjoy."

Although he returned to work, Mr. Dutremble still lived with the effects of heart disease. He became tired more easily and needed rest. He was more sensitive to the weather. He got cold more quickly in the winter and hotter during the summer.

Three years after Mr. Dutremble's heart attack, he suffered a small stroke. This happened when the blood supply to part of his brain was blocked, possibly by a blood clot in an **artery** leading to his brain.

Mr. Dutremble was partially paralyzed for several days before the effects of the stroke wore off. Since then he has had no more heart problems.

Mr. Dutremble takes two types of medicine that help his heart. One medicine slows his heart so it doesn't work so hard. The other helps his body get rid of extra fluid. Sometimes people with weak hearts have trouble with too much fluid in their bodies.

Mr. Dutremble's doctor told him to exercise regularly and to eat a healthy diet. Mr. Dutremble says he tries to do this, but he doesn't always.

Mr. Dutremble has stopped smoking, which doctors believe may have helped cause his heart attack. He also tries to keep his weight at a healthy level. When he can, he likes to bicycle and hike and go camping and swimming.

"It has not held me back," he said of his heart disease.

The fear he felt about dying after his operation has faded. He says he sometimes feels "invincible."

Chapter 2

How the Heart Works

The human body is made of trillions of cells. Each cell has a specific job to do. Some, like muscle cells, move arms and legs. Others, like the cells in the stomach and intestines, help digest food. Each cell is like a mini-factory, making a product or doing a job for the body. Like a factory, each cell needs energy to work. Each cell also needs to get rid of waste products. The **circulatory system** takes care of both needs. It brings nutrients and oxygen to each cell. Nutrients come from food and provide the energy needed by the body. The circulatory system also carries away waste products, like carbon dioxide.

The circulatory system is made up of the heart, the blood vessels (tubes that move blood from the heart to the various parts of the body and then back to the heart), and the blood. Vessels that carry blood away from the heart are called arteries. Vessels that return blood to the heart are called **veins**.

The artery leaving the heart is the **aorta**. The aorta branches into smaller arteries. These arteries then branch into smaller vessels called **arterioles**, which branch into still smaller vessels called **capillaries**. Capillaries are so tiny that ten of them bunched together are only as thick as a human hair. Capillaries have very thin sides that allow nutrients and oxygen to flow out of the capillaries and into the body cells. They also allow waste products to flow into the blood.

Inside the blood vessels are blood cells. The most common of these are called red blood cells. These help carry oxygen to the other cells. The blood cells travel in a watery fluid called **plasma**, which also carries nutrients to the body cells.

Once the blood has been brought to the cells, it must return to the heart. Its journey back begins through tiny vessels, called **venules**, that are linked to the capillaries. The venules then join to form veins. The body's two largest veins, the superior vena cava and the inferior vena cava, return blood to the heart. If this whole network of blood vessels were stretched out, it would cover more than sixty thousand miles.

After the blood returns to the heart, it is pumped through a second smaller

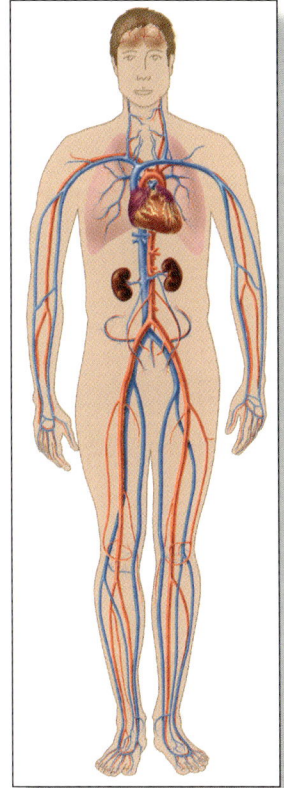

This is the circulatory system. Arteries (shown in red) and veins (shown in blue) are connected by tiny capillaries.

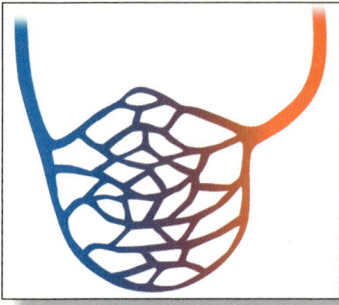

Clusters of capillaries connect the arteries and the veins.

loop into the lungs. Inside the lungs, the network of arterioles branches into clusters of capillaries that surround tiny sacs filled with air. Here the red blood cells release the carbon dioxide from the body cells and absorb oxygen from the air. After leaving the lungs, the blood returns to the heart. Full of oxygen, the blood gets pumped through the body again.

The Heart

The organ that drives this whole system is the heart. In an adult, the heart is about the size of two clenched fists. It has four chambers. The top two are called atria. Each **atrium** collects blood to be pumped. The bottom two are called **ventricles**. These do the hard work of pumping.

The heart is divided into two sides. The right side pumps blood into the lungs, where it gets oxygen. The left side pumps blood through the body. Between the two sides is a wall called the **septum**.

One-way valves connect the chambers of the heart. These valves help keep blood flowing in one direction.

The heart is the body's hardest-working organ. It beats between sixty and one hundred times a minute. That's more than 31 million times in a year. In that time it pumps more than 4 million gallons of blood.

In order for the heart to work properly, the beating of its four chambers must be coordinated, just as an orchestra needs to be coordinated to produce good music.

The heartbeat is controlled by electricity. A special group of cells in the heart sends out electrical impulses. This group is called the **sinoatrial node**. The electrical impulses cause the ventricles of the heart to contract. When this happens, blood is pumped.

The sinoatrial node can speed or slow the heartbeat, depending on the needs of the body. If a healthy person is resting, the heart beats slowly. If a person begins to move or exercise, the heart beats more quickly. The amount of electricity produced by the sinoatrial node is very small. It would not even turn on a tiny light bulb.

The Blood Supply

Thousands of gallons of blood flow through the heart every day. But the heart cannot use this blood to function. It needs its own supply, as do all the other organs in the body. The heart's blood supply comes from the coronary arteries. These arteries come from the aorta. They spread out over the heart and bring blood, with its load of oxygen, to the heart muscle cells.

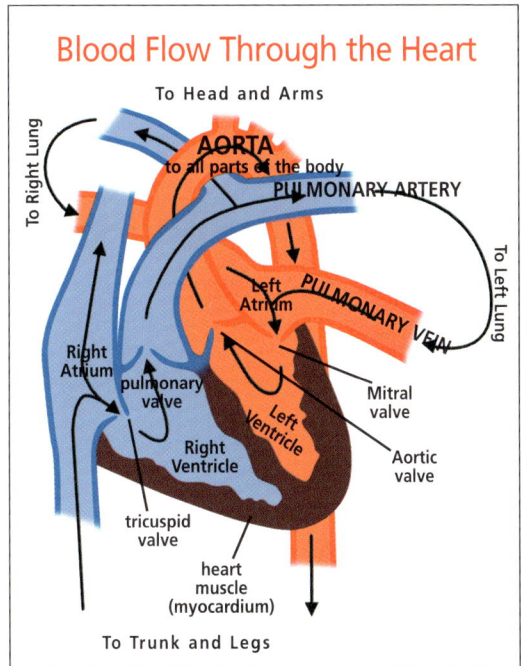

Blood Flow Through the Heart

To Head and Arms

To Right Lung

AORTA
to all parts of the body

PULMONARY ARTERY

To Left Lung

Left Atrium

PULMONARY VEIN

Right Atrium

pulmonary valve

Mitral valve

Right Ventricle

Left Ventricle

Aortic valve

tricuspid valve

heart muscle (myocardium)

To Trunk and Legs

Chapter 3

Types of Heart Disease

Every year in the United States, about 1.1 million people like Mr. Dutremble suffer heart attacks. More than four hundred seventy-five thousand of those people die. That's more than thirteen hundred a day. Cardiovascular diseases—those that affect the heart and the blood flow—struck more than 58 million Americans and killed almost one million people in 1996. That makes cardiovascular disease the number one killer of Americans.

A heart attack occurs when the blood vessels that feed the heart become clogged with fatty particles called **plaque**. When this happens, the heart muscle cannot get enough blood. Without enough blood, the muscle cells cannot get enough oxygen. They begin to die. This can take place very quickly.

The medical term for heart attack is **myocardial infarction**. The expression means "death of the heart muscle."

When the muscle cells die, they send out signals of pain.

A heart attack is extremely painful. Some patients who have had heart attacks say it is the worst pain they have ever felt. Some have said it felt as if an elephant were standing on their chest.

If enough muscle cells die, the heart's beating may be affected. The heart may stop beating. If this happens, the person can die.

If the blood vessels serving the heart are only partially blocked, a person can have **angina pectoris**. Angina is like a small heart attack. It occurs if the heart doesn't get enough blood when a person is exercising or doing other strenuous activity. Unlike the pain of a heart attack, angina pain stops when the person stops exercising. The American Heart Association (AHA) says that more than 6 million Americans suffer from angina.

Heart attack and angina are the most common types of heart disease. But there are many other kinds. In some cases, a disease may make it hard for the heart to work. This can weaken the heart over many years. This is sometimes called **heart failure**.

A weak heart cannot pump blood as well as a strong heart. This deficiency affects the rest of the body. People who have a weak heart may feel tired because their organs are not receiving enough blood. They may have trouble breathing. Fluid may build up in their bodies.

Other diseases can affect the blood vessels. The plaque that blocks heart vessels can also block other blood vessels. If these vessels lead to other organs, the organs can die or become damaged, just like the heart.

How plaque forms is not completely known. Most scientists believe the process is a lifelong one that begins in childhood. They think that fatty material in the blood-stream becomes attached to the lining of the blood vessel. When this happens, fibers may grow out of the blood vessel lining and surround the material. This forms the plaque. Over many years the plaque may grow until it blocks the entire blood vessel.

New studies suggest that the body's immune system may also be involved in the production of plaque. This theory is still being examined.

As the plaque accumulates, the blood vessels become stiff and hard. This process is called hardening of the arteries, or **arteriosclerosis**.

Heart Rhythms

Other heart diseases affect the way the heart beats. They may cause the heart to beat too quickly or too slowly. They may also disrupt the orderly beating of the heart. This condition is called **arrhythmia**.

More than 4 million people in America have some kind of heart rhythm disorder.

Hypertension

Like water flowing through a pipe, blood circulating in a body is under pressure. When that pressure is higher than normal, a person has high blood pressure, or **hypertension**.

Blood pressure is measured with an instrument called a **sphygmomanometer**. It is used to measure the blood pressure when the heart is working and when it is resting. The resting pressure is called the **diastolic** reading. The normal reading for an adult at rest is eighty and for a child six to nine, a normal at-rest reading is seventy-eight or below. A normal reading for children ten to twelve is no greater than eighty-two.

When the heart is at work, the pressure is called **systolic**. The normal systolic reading for an adult is one hundred twenty. Children six to

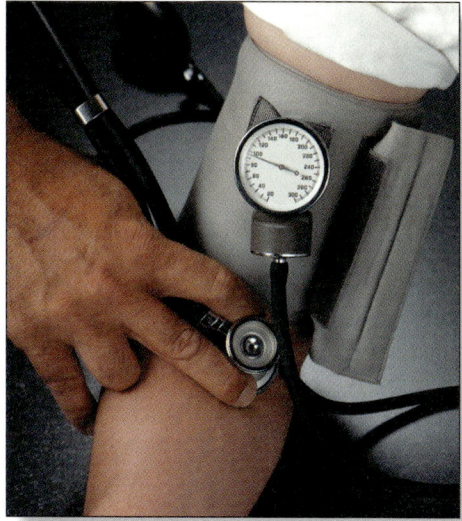

A sphygmomanometer and a stethoscope are used to measure blood pressure.

nine should have a reading no greater than one hundred twenty-two; those ten to twelve should not exceed one hundred twenty-six. The two readings are written together like this: systolic/diastolic, or 120/80.

Hypertension affects about 50 million Americans. Almost 3 million of them are young people between ages six and seventeen. Most people with hypertension do not feel anything. Some may have headaches or feel dizzy.

Hypertension is a serious disease that can cause many problems. It speeds the processes that cause arteries to harden or become clogged. Because of this, it can lead to eye damage, strokes, heart attacks, and heart failure. High blood pressure also makes the kidneys work harder. This can cause kidney failure. Almost forty-two thousand Americans died from high blood pressure in 1996. Doctors don't know what causes most cases of this condition.

Rheumatic Heart Disease

Before penicillin was discovered, many people suffered from a disease called rheumatic heart disease. This disease was caused by the same bacteria that cause strep throat. Some people infected by the bacteria got rheumatic fever. This made the body's joints swell and also caused a rash and a fever. The bacteria can also damage the valves of the heart. This damage can prevent the heart from working properly. Eventually it can cause heart failure.

Today penicillin and other drugs fight bacteria. These medications prevent most cases of rheumatic fever. If a person does get rheumatic heart disease, doctors can replace damaged heart valves.

About 1.8 million people in the United States have rheumatic heart disease. In 1996, about five thousand people died from this disease.

Stroke

Sometimes the arteries that bring blood to the brain can become narrowed by deposits or be suddenly blocked by a blood clot. If this happens, a part of the brain does not receive enough oxygen and may die. This condition is called a stroke.

Strokes can be deadly. In 1996 the American Heart Association reported that 159,942 people died from strokes. Stroke victims who survive may lose control of part of their bodies. They may be partially paralyzed. They may have trouble speaking or understanding other people. They may also have trouble seeing.

Patients can learn to walk again by doing physical therapy.

With special treatment, many stroke patients learn to walk and talk again. Physical therapists help patients exercise and learn how to use their limbs again. A therapist may also help patients learn to speak clearly. Other therapists can help patients learn to adjust to the effects of their illness. They show patients how to use a wheelchair and dress themselves.

The American Heart Association reported in 1999 that about 4.4 million Americans were still alive after suffering a stroke.

Congenital Defects

The heart begins as a simple tube in a baby growing inside the mother. As the heart develops, the tube bends and loops. It divides into four chambers. It connects with the rest of the circulatory system.

Sometimes something goes wrong. There may be an opening between two chambers that shouldn't be there. A valve may not open or close properly. In some cases, the

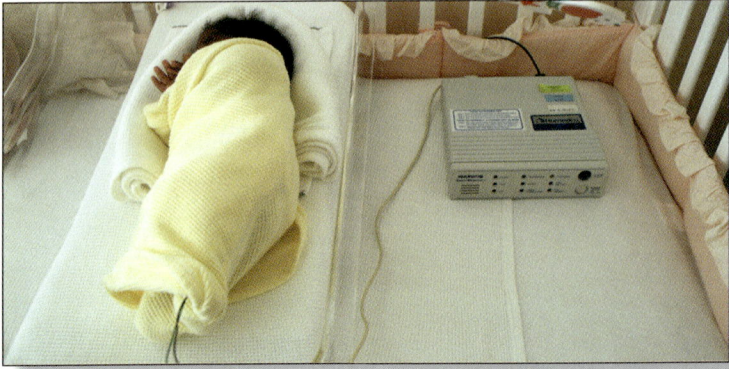

A heart-lung monitor keeps track of a baby's heartbeat and breathing. In the United States, thirty-two thousand babies are born each year with heart defects.

large blood vessels leaving the heart may be switched. These problems that affect the developing baby are called **congenital heart defects**.

In the United States, thirty-two thousand babies are born each year with heart defects. Of these, about forty-eight hundred die. But many live. In 1996, the American Heart Association said that about 1 million people born with heart defects were still alive.

The most common defect is a hole between the lower chambers (ventricles) of the heart. In many cases, the defect may not cause serious problems. Or the defect may not be noticed until the child becomes an adult. In some cases, though, the defect may prevent the blood from reaching the baby's lungs. If this happens, the blood may not receive enough oxygen and the baby's skin and lips may look blue. Or, if a heart valve is seriously damaged, the heart cannot pump blood efficiently.

Many defects can be fixed through surgery. A surgeon can patch improper openings or switch arteries to their proper positions. In rare cases, surgeons may operate while the developing baby is still in the mother's womb.

Chapter 4

Causes of Heart Disease

At the start of the twenty-first century, diseases of the heart and blood vessels killed more Americans than any other disease, according to the American Heart Association. In the United States, one in five people has some form of heart disease. That's more than the number suffering from cancer or AIDS.

The AHA estimates that diseases of the heart and circulation system will cost $326.6 billion in the year 2000. This figure includes the cost of medical care, medicine, and days lost from work because people are disabled.

The good news is that people with heart disease are less likely than in the past to die from the disease. People live longer today, and because of this, more people have heart disease. But when the figures are adjusted for age, death rates from heart disease and stroke have dropped 60 percent since 1950. Advances in medicine help more and more people survive heart attacks. And education and

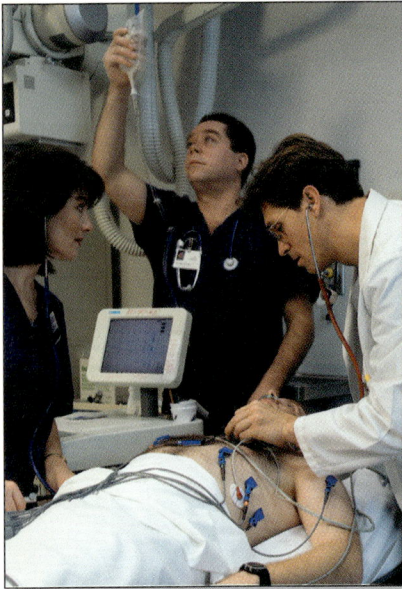

A medical team checks a patient before surgery.

prevention measures help more people avoid the disease altogether.

Heart disease has probably been around as long as people have been on earth. As early as 400 B.C. Greek doctors described how the heart worked. In 1628, William Harvey, an English doctor, published a paper describing the body's circulatory system. Other doctors at that time did not believe him. Most people thought the blood flow was controlled by eating. They thought blood ebbed and flowed like the tides in the ocean.

The first successful heart operation was done in 1896. A German doctor repaired a bullet wound in the heart of a soldier. The heart-lung machine was invented in the mid-1950s. This machine took over the job of circulating blood through the body and of giving it oxygen. It allowed doctors to stop the heart during surgery.

The first bypass operation was performed in 1967 by René Favaloro, a doctor at The Cleveland Clinic. That same year South African surgeon Christiaan Barnard became the first to transplant a heart from one human being to another.

Today, doctors around the world perform bypass operations every day. Heart transplants have become much more common than they were two decades ago. Some doctors are even working on mechanical hearts. But scientists still don't have all the answers. Why do some people get heart disease and others with similar lifestyles avoid heart problems? Although doctors have clues, there is still much to learn about the disease and what causes it.

Causes

Scientists don't know exactly how heart disease starts. But they have some theories. One theory is that a chemical process called oxidation causes **cholesterol** in the blood to turn into plaque. Oxidation is the same process that causes metal to rust. In 1993, one study found that people who took vitamin E regularly had a lower risk of heart disease. Some researchers believe this may be because vitamin E blocks the oxidation process. Other studies are needed, however, to investigate exactly how vitamin E affects the body and to prove whether it truly can reduce the risk of heart disease.

Another theory is that a virus like the one that causes cold sores may cause plaque to form in the blood vessels. Some scientists believe that the virus may start a reaction that causes blood to clot and form plaque. Bacteria, such as the type that causes gum disease, may have a similar effect in the body, according to some scientists.

In the past fifty years, scientists have conducted thousands of studies to find the cause of heart disease. One of the first studies, the Framingham Study, began in 1948. Doctors examined fifty-two hundred men and women in Framingham, Massachusetts, over a long period of time. They were still being studied in the year 2000.

Every two years doctors examined the people in the study and asked them questions about how they lived and what they ate. The doctors watched to see who among the study's participants got heart disease and who did not.

From that study and many others like it, doctors conclude that the way people live helps determine whether they get heart disease. High-fat foods, lack of exercise, diabetes, and smoking may all increase the chances of heart disease. People with high blood pressure and high cholesterol levels run a higher risk of getting heart disease. Doctors also believe heredity may play a part. People are more likely to get heart disease if someone else in their family has had heart disease.

Stress has been linked to heart disease in several studies. In 1997, scientists from the Public Health Institute in Berkeley, California, studied more than ten thousand British men and women who worked for the government. Over a period of five years, the researchers asked workers to talk about how much stress they felt on the job. The researchers found that workers who felt greater levels of stress also had higher rates of heart disease.

In 1999, a team of researchers at Vrije University in Amsterdam conducted a similar study of more than one hundred workers. In this study, however, the researchers took blood samples and measured the amount of clot-dissolving chemicals that were in the blood. These chemicals can help prevent heart attacks. The researchers found that workers who reported high levels of stress had lower levels of the clot-dissolving chemicals.

Doctors have found that heart disease is more common in older people and that men are more likely to have heart disease than women. Recently, however, more women have been diagnosed with heart disease, and it has become the leading cause of death for women as well as men. Doctors have also learned that bald men have a higher chance of having a heart attack than others. These factors cannot be changed. A person can't do anything about being old or bald. But some things can be changed.

Smoking

People who smoke are much more likely to suffer a heart attack and are also at greater risk of dying after a heart attack. The deaths of one in five people who die from cardiovascular disease are caused by smoking, according to the American Heart Association.

Studies show smoking speeds the process that causes arteries to clog. It also speeds another process that causes artery walls to harden. Both of these conditions—clogged arteries and hardened artery walls—make it more difficult for the heart to work and can lead to heart disease.

The gases inhaled by smokers damage the lining of blood vessels. Smoking also causes an increase in blood-clotting material in the bloodstream. These clots can get stuck in blood vessels that are already too narrow.

High Blood Pressure

Studies show that people with high blood pressure are more likely to have heart disease. High blood pressure can be controlled by medicines. Doctors also tell patients with high blood pressure to eat less salt, reduce the amount of alcohol they drink, lose weight, and exercise regularly. All these can help lower blood pressure.

Cholesterol

You may have heard a lot of bad things about cholesterol. Cholesterol is a type of fat found in the bloodstream. Many people try to avoid eating foods that are high in cholesterol. But the body needs cholesterol in small amounts and even produces its own. The body uses it to help produce the walls of cells. It also helps create hormones and a substance that helps digest food.

Too much cholesterol can be bad, however. The body deposits excess cholesterol on the lining of the blood vessels, where it forms plaque. If enough plaque builds up, the blood vessel becomes blocked. If this happens in an artery supplying blood to the heart, the person can have angina or a heart attack.

Like blood pressure, cholesterol can be controlled by medicines and diet. Doctors tell patients to eat low-fat foods, lose weight, and get regular exercise.

Exercise

Scientists believe that regular exercise may reduce the risk of heart disease. They are not completely sure why, but they do have some ideas. They know that exercise helps reduce obesity, which is linked to heart disease. Exercise can also help people lower their blood pressure and reduce cholesterol levels.

Chapter 5

Diagnosing Heart Disease

When a person with a medical problem comes to a doctor, the doctor must make a diagnosis. That means the doctor must discover what is causing the patient's problem. The doctor conducts tests and asks the patient questions about the problem. When the doctor knows what the cause is, he or she can decide how to treat the illness or condition.

In heart disease, a doctor can run many tests to find out what is wrong with the patient. The first thing a doctor does is check the patient's medical history. The doctor has the patient describe his or her symptoms and when they occur. The doctor asks if the patient has had heart problems before. The doctor also asks if anyone in the patient's family has had heart disease.

Then the doctor gives the patient a thorough physical examination. The doctor tests the patient's blood pressure and listens to the patient's heart through a stethoscope.

Sometimes the doctor can hear an irregular heartbeat. The doctor may also draw blood from the patient. The blood is tested to check the patient's cholesterol level.

Doctors can learn a lot from these simple tests. Sometimes they reveal that the patient's medical problem is not related to the heart. But if the doctor believes that the problem is caused by the heart, he or she may run more tests. These tests tell the doctor what is wrong with the patient's heart.

The EKG

One of the simplest tests for heart disease can be performed by a machine called an **electrocardiograph**. This machine measures the electrical activity of the heart. The machine prints a record called an **electrocardiogram**, or EKG. It can tell a doctor if the heart is beating properly and also if the patient has had a recent heart attack. Sometimes a patient may think a mild heart attack is only indigestion or another minor problem.

Electrodes are placed on each arm and leg

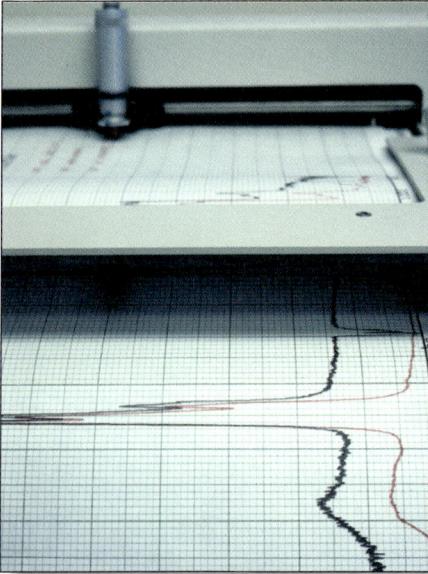

An electrocardiograph measures the electrical activity of the heart.

and at six points on the chest over the heart area. These electrodes pick up the electrical activity of the heart. The signals are sent to a machine that records them on a moving strip of paper. This produces a wavelike image of the heart's rhythm. The doctor can compare this image with that of a healthy heart.

A portable EKG machine can record the heart rhythm of a patient who is moving. In this test, the patient carries a device like a tape recorder, wearing it at home for twenty-four hours. During this time the machine records signals from the heart. When the test is finished, the machine plays back the signals for the doctor to examine.

Chest X-ray

An X-ray is a picture of the inside of the body. It is taken by a special camera that sends energy through the body. Some of the energy is absorbed by the body's parts. The rest of the energy goes through the body and is recorded on a special film. An X-ray of the chest can help show an enlarged heart.

Echocardiography

Echocardiography is a technique for examining the internal structure of the heart using sound. It is one of the most common tests performed by heart doctors.

In this test, a doctor or a technician places a special device on the patient's chest. The device sends out sound waves. They bounce off the heart and other organs in the chest and are recorded on the machine. These waves are translated by the machine into a picture of the heart called an echocardiogram.

This picture can show the size of the heart and the thickness of the heart muscle. It can also help measure the amount of blood flowing through the heart. A heart that is enlarged, muscle that is too thin, or blood flow that is restricted are all indications of heart disease.

Exercise Stress Testing

Sometimes patients have chest pain only when they are exercising. To check this, a doctor may run an exercise stress test. This is an EKG that is done while the patient is walking on a treadmill or riding a stationary bike. It measures the heart's rhythm while the heart is working hard.

Doctors usually give this test to find out when a patient's chest pain occurs. If it happens during exercise, there is a greater chance the pain is related to the heart.

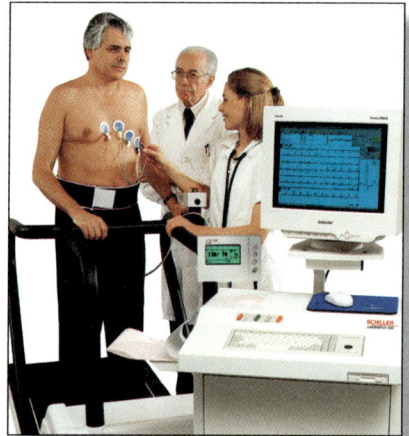

A patient undergoes a stress test. An electrocardiograph measures his heartbeat while he exercises on a treadmill.

High-Tech Scanning

Doctors can also use scanning machines that create three-dimensional pictures of the inside of the body. These pictures are used to study the heart and blood vessels. The machines are called computed tomography (CT) scanners and magnetic resonance imaging (MRI) scanners. Like an X-ray camera, they use a form of energy to create pictures. Besides giving doctors a better idea of what the heart looks like, these scans can also measure blood flow.

In the late 1990s, researchers used a special type of CT scan to identify some people at risk of developing heart disease but who had not yet had any heart problems. The scans, still in the experimental stage, can detect calcium deposits, which are among the first signs that arteries are becoming clogged. Scientists are also experimenting with MRI scans to do a similar procedure.

Nuclear Testing

Doctors use nuclear tests to see the heart at work. The doctor injects a small amount of a radioactive chemical called an **isotope** into the patient's bloodstream. Then, using a special camera, the doctor follows the isotope as it is carried through the circulatory system. This test lets the doctor "see" the patient's blood as it flows through the vessels.

By using one type of isotope, the doctor can watch as blood moves through the heart. He or she can measure how much blood the heart pumps. The heart needs to pump enough blood to keep the body healthy. But if the test shows that the heart is pumping less blood than it should, something is wrong.

Another kind of isotope is absorbed by the heart. By using this isotope, the doctor can see how much of the heart's muscle is healthy. If the doctor sees a lot of the isotope in the heart, he or she knows the muscle is getting enough blood. But if little of the isotope is absorbed, the doctor knows the heart muscle may not be getting enough blood or may be damaged.

Another kind of nuclear test, called the **thallium** stress test, is done while the patient is exercising. During this test, the patient walks on a treadmill to get his or her heart beating faster. When the heart is beating at a certain rate, the doctor injects a radioactive isotope called thallium into the bloodstream. Then, using a special camera, the doctor tracks the thallium. This tells the doctor how much blood is reaching the heart muscle.

Cardiac Catheterization

Sometimes a doctor inserts an instrument inside the heart to get a highly accurate picture. To do this, the doctor uses a **catheter**—a long, thin, flexible hollow tube. The doctor inserts the tube into an artery in the patient's leg. Then he or she slides the tube through the artery until the tube reaches and enters the heart.

Once the catheter is in the heart, the doctor attaches the catheter to an instrument that measures blood pressure inside the heart.

The doctor also injects a special dye through the catheter. This dye can be seen on an X-ray camera. The doctor watches to see how the dye flows through the heart. The dye shows if the heart is blocked by valves that aren't working properly. It also shows if the arteries to the heart are blocked. The dye test is called **angiography**.

Chapter 6

Treatment of Heart Disease

Researchers have found many new ways to treat heart disease. New surgical techniques and medicines help people with heart disease live healthy lives, as does Dennis Dutremble, the teacher and state senator you read about in Chapter 1.

A person who is having a heart attack must be taken quickly to a hospital for treatment. Speed in getting help is important, because a heart attack causes heart muscle cells to die. The longer the wait for medical attention, the more cells die. As cells die, the heart becomes weaker and less able to do its job.

Sometimes a patient's heart stops beating. Rescuers perform **cardiopulmonary resuscitation (CPR)** to keep the patient alive. Using CPR, a rescuer breathes into the patient's mouth and pumps the person's heart by pushing on his or her chest until medical help arrives. Anyone can learn CPR, which is taught by many groups.

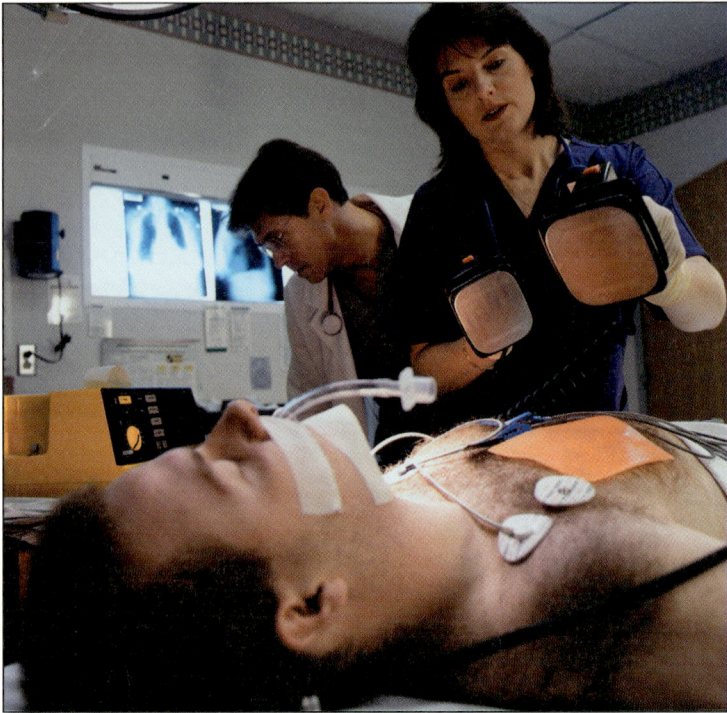

A medical team uses a defibrillator on a heart patient in an emergency room.

Rescuers may also try to restart a patient's heart using a device called a **defibrillator**. This machine sends a surge of electricity through the patient's heart to restart the heart's normal rhythm. Because defibrillators have been shown to save lives, many organizations and companies have small versions of the machines and have trained their employees to use them.

Once the patient is at a hospital, doctors swing into action. The most important thing is to make sure the patient's heart is beating steadily. First the patient is hooked to an EKG. Doctors quickly review the patient's medical history and the EKG results.

Doctors may inject a special type of medicine into the patient. This medicine is known as a **thrombolytic**, or clot-dissolving, agent. It can dissolve clots that are blocking blood flow to the heart. Doctors may also inject medicine to bring the heart's rhythm under control.

Drug Treatment

Once the patient is stable and not at risk of dying, the doctor needs to figure out what kind of treatment is needed. If the heart attack was not severe and did not damage the heart, the patient may only need to rest. The doctor may tell the patient to change diet, stop smoking, and get more exercise. The doctor may also prescribe medicines to make it easier for the heart to work.

Nitroglycerin, one of the most common heart medicines, causes blood vessels to expand. This increases blood flow through the vessels and eases the heart's job. If the patient has high blood pressure, the doctor may prescribe medicine to treat that condition.

Balloon Angioplasty

If the heart disease is severe, medicine may not be enough. The heart may be too seriously damaged or the blood vessels too blocked.

One way to open a blood vessel is to thread a catheter into the clogged vessel. At the end of the catheter is a tiny balloon. When the catheter is in the blocked area, the doctor inflates the balloon. The pressure from the balloon presses the fatty deposits against the wall of the artery. This medical procedure, called **balloon angioplasty**, opens the way for blood.

Scientists are studying another device that uses a laser beam instead of a balloon. The laser sends out tiny bursts of energy that vaporize the plaque blockages.

Another device used in heart treatments is a tiny, high-speed drill. This shaves the plaque blockages from the inside of the vessel. The drill is threaded into the vessel along a guide wire. The doctor may insert a tiny metal mesh tube called a **stent** inside the artery. This helps keep the artery open, preventing plaque buildup and allowing the blood to flow freely.

Open-Heart Surgery

Sometimes the blood vessels are too blocked for angioplasty to work. Then doctors have to perform surgery to create a new route for blood to get to the heart.

This surgery is called a bypass operation because it provides a detour around the blocked arteries. You may hear people talk about double and triple bypasses. This means the surgeon had to find routes around two or three blocked arteries.

The bypass operation has become very common in the United States. In 1996, surgeons performed bypass operations on an estimated 366,000 patients.

The bypass operation is done during open-heart surgery. The patient is put to sleep, and the surgeon opens his or her chest. Once the heart is exposed, the patient is hooked to a heart-lung machine. Then the heart is stopped by an injection of a drug or by electric shock.

The surgeon takes a blood vessel from the leg or the chest of the patient and uses it to build a new route around the blocked artery. The surgeon uses tiny stitches to sew one end of the vein onto the aorta and the other end of the vein onto the coronary artery. A special headlight and a magnifying glass help the surgeon to see the area clearly. Mr. Dutremble had this kind of operation.

When the bypass operation is completed, the patient's heart is restarted and the heart-lung machine removed. The surgeon closes the patient's chest and sews the breast bone back together with stainless steel wire.

Open-heart surgery is also used to replace damaged valves in the heart. The valves are replaced with mechanical devices that do the same job. Some valves may be replaced by parts from a pig's heart or from someone who has died.

Someday surgeons may be able to replace damaged valves with new ones grown from a heart patient's own cells. Researchers have

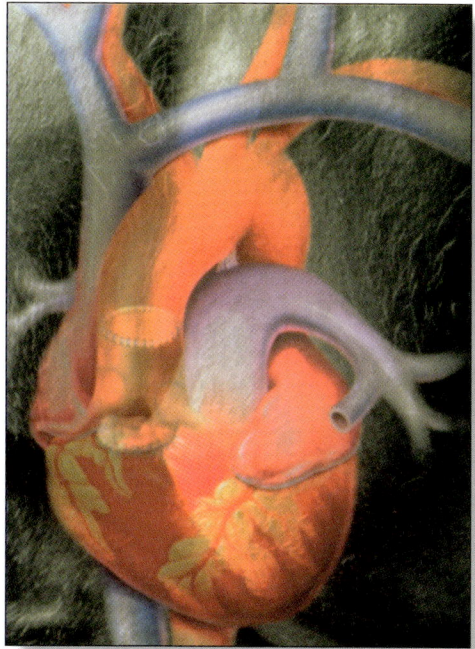

This is how a heart valve is positioned inside the heart.

been able to grow new valves in a test tube. Using cells removed from a lamb's healthy artery, the scientists were able to fashion a valve from the growing cells. This has not yet been tried with human cells.

Keyhole Surgery

In some cases, doctors can operate on the heart without opening the patient's chest. The doctor cuts several small holes in the patient's chest, then inserts a tiny camera and special

An artificial heart valve.

surgical instruments. The camera allows the doctor to see what he or she is doing on a television screen. This type of operation is called **keyhole surgery**. Doctors hope someday to be able to use remote control devices to perform this type of delicate surgery inside the body.

Pacemakers

If a patient's heart is not beating properly, the doctor may install a **pacemaker**. This device sends out electrical signals that help keep the heart beating properly. It is used when the heart's own electrical-impulse system is not working.

In this operation the surgeon threads two wires into the heart and attaches them to the chambers. The other end of the wires is attached to the pacemaker. The pacemaker, about the size of a silver dollar, is positioned under the skin of the chest.

The pacemaker is run by special batteries that last for many years. When the batteries need replacing, the doctor must remove the pacemaker and install new ones.

Another type of pacemaker performs the same job as a

defibrillator. Like the regular pacemaker, this device is implanted in the chest. But instead of sending a steady rhythm, it works only when the patient's heart beats irregularly. Then the device sends out a jolt of electricity to get the heart beating in a normal rhythm again.

Transplants

In some cases, the patient's heart may be too damaged to save—because of coronary artery disease or because of a congenital defect. In these cases, doctors may decide to perform a transplant.

In a transplant, a healthy human heart is taken from a person who has died from causes not related to heart disease. The heart is put into the chest of someone with a diseased heart.

The first patients who received transplants often died because their bodies rejected the hearts. Since then, doctors have discovered medicines to help prevent rejection. Now, 65 percent of heart transplant patients live more than five years after their operations.

One of the biggest problems with transplants is to find a heart that matches the patient's. Sometimes the search can take many months. A person with a diseased heart may not have that long to live.

To solve this problem, scientists are studying ways to make an artificial heart. One such heart, the Jarvik-7, has been implanted in several patients. The first person to receive a Jarvik-7 was a dentist named Barney Clark, in 1982. Clark lived for 112 days with the artificial heart but then died.

The second person to receive an artificial heart was a man named William Schroder. Schroder lived for almost two years with his heart. He was able to leave the hospital and live in a special apartment. Schroder even went fishing with his family.

The Jarvik-7 had several drawbacks, however. One of the biggest problems was that it was run by compressed air. The patient had to be hooked to an outside power supply by two large hoses. The power supply, called a Utah drive, weighed 375 pounds. Patients with the Jarvik-7 could not move around freely. They could go out for short periods with a portable power supply, though.

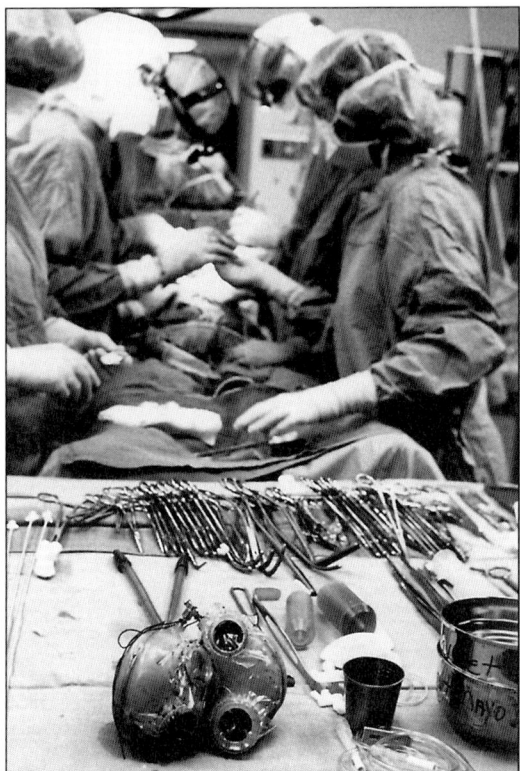

Surgeons at the Norton Audubon Heart Institute in Louisville, Kentucky, prepare to implant the Jarvik-7 artificial heart in William Schroder in 1984. The Jarvik-7 is on the table in the foreground.

An artificial heart does not work exactly like a real heart. Because of this, it can cause the patient's blood to clot. Schroder suffered several strokes because of blood clots produced by the Jarvik-7.

The artificial heart is very expensive. Doctor bills for Clark's operation were more than $250,000.

Because of the problems, doctors do not use artificial hearts as a permanent solution to heart disease. A newer version of the artificial heart is sometimes used to keep people alive while they wait for a real human heart. Scientists are still trying to build a better artificial heart.

Repair Without Surgery

Scientists are working on techniques that they hope will allow them to repair the heart without surgery. In tests, they have discovered a certain **protein** that can make the body create new blood vessels. Proteins are substances found in all living things. Tissue needs proteins to grow and repair itself. By injecting the protein into the heart, researchers hope to create new blood vessels that can replace blocked coronary arteries.

Prevention—The Best Cure

The best treatment for most heart disease is prevention. Doctors believe many people can avoid heart disease altogether by living healthier lives. Even those who inherit a weak heart can improve their chances of surviving a heart attack by taking certain precautions.

The doctor's prescription for a healthy heart—eat a healthy, low-fat diet; get regular exercise; have blood pressure and cholesterol levels checked regularly; and don't smoke. By following these rules, people may someday be able to defeat America's number one killer.

Further Reading

Arnold, Caroline. *Heart Disease*. New York: Franklin Watts, 1990.

Galperin, Anne. *Stroke & Heart Disease*. Broomall, Penn.: Chelsea House, 1991.

Hyde, Margaret O., and Elizabeth H. Forsyth. *The Disease Book*. New York: Walker & Company, 1997.

Johansson, Philip. *Heart Disease*. Berkeley Heights, N.J.: Enslow Publishers, 1998.

Parker, Steve. *Blood*. Brookfield, Conn.: Millbrook Press, Inc., 1997.

Parramon, Merce. *How Our Blood Circulates*. Broomall, Penn.: Chelsea House, 1994.

Ruiz, Andres Llamas. *Blood Circulation*. New York: Sterling Publications, 1996.

Saunderson, Jane and Andrew Farmer. *Heart & Lungs*. Mahwah, N.J.: Troll Communications, L.L.C., 1992.

Walton, Karen. *How Will They Get That Heart Down Your Throat?: A Child's View of Transplants*. Manassas, Va.: E.M Press, 1997.

For More Information

The following is a list of organizations and Internet sites that deal with heart disease.

Organizations

American Heart Association National Center
7272 Greenville Ave., Dallas, TX 75231, (800) AHA-USA1, <http://www.americanheart.org>

Heart and Stroke Foundation of Canada
222 Queen St., Suite 1402, Ottawa, Ontario K1P 5V9, (613) 569-4361, <http://www.hsf.ca>

Mended Hearts Inc.
7272 Greenville Ave., Dallas, TX 75231-4596, (214) 706-1442, (800) AHA-USA1; <http://www.mendedhearts.org>; support groups, hospital visits by volunteers.

National Heart, Lung and Blood Institute
NHLBI Information Center, P.O. Box 30105, Bethesda, MD 20824-0105, (301) 592-8573, <http://www.nhlbi.nih.gov>

National Stroke Association
96 Inverness Dr. East, Suite I, Englewood, CO 80112-5112, (303) 649-9299, (800) STROKES, <http://www.stroke.org>

Stroke Connection of the American Heart Association
7272 Greenville Ave., Dallas, TX 75231, (800) 553-6321, <http://www.healthy.net/pan/cso/cioi/Scaha.htm>

Internet Resources

<http://www.curiousheart.com>

Basic information about heart disease in everyday language, related links, and discussion group. Maintained by Curious Heart Enterprises, a nurse-owned company.

<http://sln.fi.edu/biosci/heart.html>

Exhibit of beating heart, series of videos on the heart. Operated by the Franklin Institute Science Museum.

<http://www.heartinfo.org>

Heart Information Network includes news, symptoms, studies, glossary, and questions and answers on heart disease. Maintained by the Center for Cardiovascular Education, Inc., New Providence, New Jersey.

<http://healthlink.mcw.edu/heart-disease>

Medical College of Wisconsin's HealthLink. Information on heart disease.

<http://www.allexperts.com/getExpert.asp?Category=964>

Cardiologists and others answer questions about heart attacks and heart disease. *Allexperts* was created by Steve Gordon, a lawyer and author.

<http://go.to/robertplotnek>

The story of Robert Plotnek, a child born with congenital heart defects who had a heart transplant at age nine.

<http://www.mayohealth.org/mayo/common/htm/heartpg.htm>

Experts at the Mayo Clinic Heart Resource Center offer information about heart disease, treatments, and steps to prevent heart disease.

Glossary

angina pectoris—Chest pain felt when the arteries supplying blood to the heart become blocked, reducing the amount of oxygen to the heart muscle.

angiography—The injection of a special dye into the bloodstream, which is then photographed by an X-ray camera. This procedure shows blockages in the arteries.

aorta—The large artery leaving the heart. It branches into smaller arteries that carry blood to the various parts of the body.

arrhythmia—Abnormal beating of the heart.

arteriole—A smaller branch of an artery.

arteriosclerosis—A form of coronary artery disease. It occurs when the walls of the artery become stiff and hard; also known as hardening of the arteries.

artery—A blood vessel that brings blood away from the heart to organs around the body.

atrium—One of the two upper chambers on the right and left of the heart. Each atrium acts as a collecting area for blood about to be pumped by the heart.

balloon angioplasty—A method of opening clogged arteries by inserting a tiny deflated balloon into the blood vessel and inflating it inside the blocked area.

bypass operation—Surgery in which a doctor uses a vein from another part of the body to build a detour around a blocked artery. Sometimes, detours are made around more than one artery.

capillaries—Tiny blood vessels that form a network which brings blood directly to body cells. Capillaries form a bridge between arteries and veins.

cardiopulmonary resuscitation (CPR)—A combination of chest compression and mouth-to-mouth breathing that can keep alive a person whose heart has stopped.

catheter—A long, thin, flexible hollow tube.

cholesterol—A fatlike substance in the bloodstream. Small amounts of it are used by the body to produce cell walls. Large amounts may cause plaque to form.

circulatory system—The system of arteries, veins, and the heart that provides blood to all parts of the body.

congenital heart defects—Problems that affect the heart of a developing baby still inside the mother.

defibrillator—A machine that sends an electrical current into the heart; used in emergencies to restart the heart.

diastolic—Refers to the resting phase of the heartbeat.

echocardiography—A technique for examining the internal structure of the heart using sound.

electrocardiogram (EKG)—The record of the heart's electrical activity.

electrocardiograph—A piece of medical equipment that measures the heart's electrical activity.

heart failure—The loss of strength of a diseased heart.

hypertension—High blood pressure.

isotope—A radioactive chemical that can be injected into the bloodstream and then traced using a special camera.

keyhole surgery—Heart surgery performed through tiny openings in the chest, using tiny instruments.

myocardial infarction—A heart attack. It means "death of the heart muscle."

nitroglycerin—Medicine for angina. It relaxes blood vessels and makes it easier for the heart to pump blood.

pacemaker—A battery-operated device connected to the heart that provides a regular pulse of electricity. It helps regulate the heart's rhythm.

plaque—Fatty particles that are deposited on the inner wall of blood vessels.

plasma—A watery fluid in the bloodstream that carries blood cells and other cells through the body.

protein—A substance found in all living things. Tissue needs protein to grow and repair itself.

septum—A wall that divides the two sides of the heart.

sinoatrial node—A cluster of cells that sends out electrical impulses which regulate the heartbeat.

sphygmomanometer—A device used to measure blood pressure when the heart is working and at rest.

stent—A tiny metal mesh tube placed inside the artery to help keep it open so blood can flow through freely.

stroke—A condition occurring when blood flow to a part of the brain stops or when bleeding occurs in the brain.

systolic—Refers to the pumping phase of the heartbeat.

thallium—A radioactive isotope that can be injected into the bloodstream and used to study the heart's blood flow.

thrombolytic—Medicine used to dissolve blood clots.

vein—A blood vessel that brings blood to the heart from organs around the body.

ventricle—One of the two lower and larger chambers on the right and left of the heart. They are responsible for pumping blood throughout the body and to the lungs.

venule—A small vein that connects a larger vein with a capillary.

Index